Pterodactyl!

Velociraptor!

Rock!

Dimetrodon!

This BOOK, BOOK, BOOK
belongs to:
Muhlenberg County Libraries
108 E. Broad St.
Central City, Kentucky 42330

DATE DUE

DISCARD

Apatos...

Triceratops!

For
CASEY!
CASEY!
CASEY!

MARGARET K. McELDERRY BOOKS • An imprint of Simon & Schuster Children's Publishing Division • 1230 Avenue of the Americas, New York, New York 10020 • Copyright © 2015 by Steven Weinberg • All rights reserved, including the right of reproduction in whole or in part in any form. • MARGARET K. McELDERRY BOOKS is a trademark of Simon & Schuster, Inc. • For information about special discounts for bulk purchases, please contact Simon & Schuster Special Sales at 1-866-506-1949 or business@simonandschuster.com. • The Simon & Schuster Speakers Bureau can bring authors to your live event. For more information or to book an event, contact the Simon & Schuster Speakers Bureau at 1-866-248-3049 or visit our website at www.simonspeakers.com. • Book design by Steven Weinberg and Lauren Rille • The text for this book is set in Avenir. • The illustrations for this book are rendered in watercolor and digitally. • Manufactured in China • 1114 SCP • Library of Congress Cataloging-in-Publication Data • Weinberg, Steven, 1984– author, illustrator. • Rex finds an egg! egg! egg! / Steven Weinberg. — First edition. • p. cm. • Summary: Rex, a tyrannosaurus, finds an egg and loves it enough to save it from a volcano that is about to erupt, protecting it as he runs, falls, splashes, tumbles, and more on the way to his nest. • ISBN 978-1-4814-0308-5 (hardcover) • ISBN 978-1-4814-0309-2 (eBook) • [1. Eggs—Fiction. 2. Tyrannosaurus rex—Fiction. 3. Dinosaurs—Fiction.] I. Title. • PZ7.W436347Rex 2015 • [E]—dc23 • 2014024232 • 2 4 6 8 10 9 7 5 3 1

FIRST EDITION

STEVEN WEINBERG

Rex Finds an
Egg!
Egg!
Egg!

Margaret K. McElderry Books • New York London Toronto Sydney New Delhi

Now he must . . .

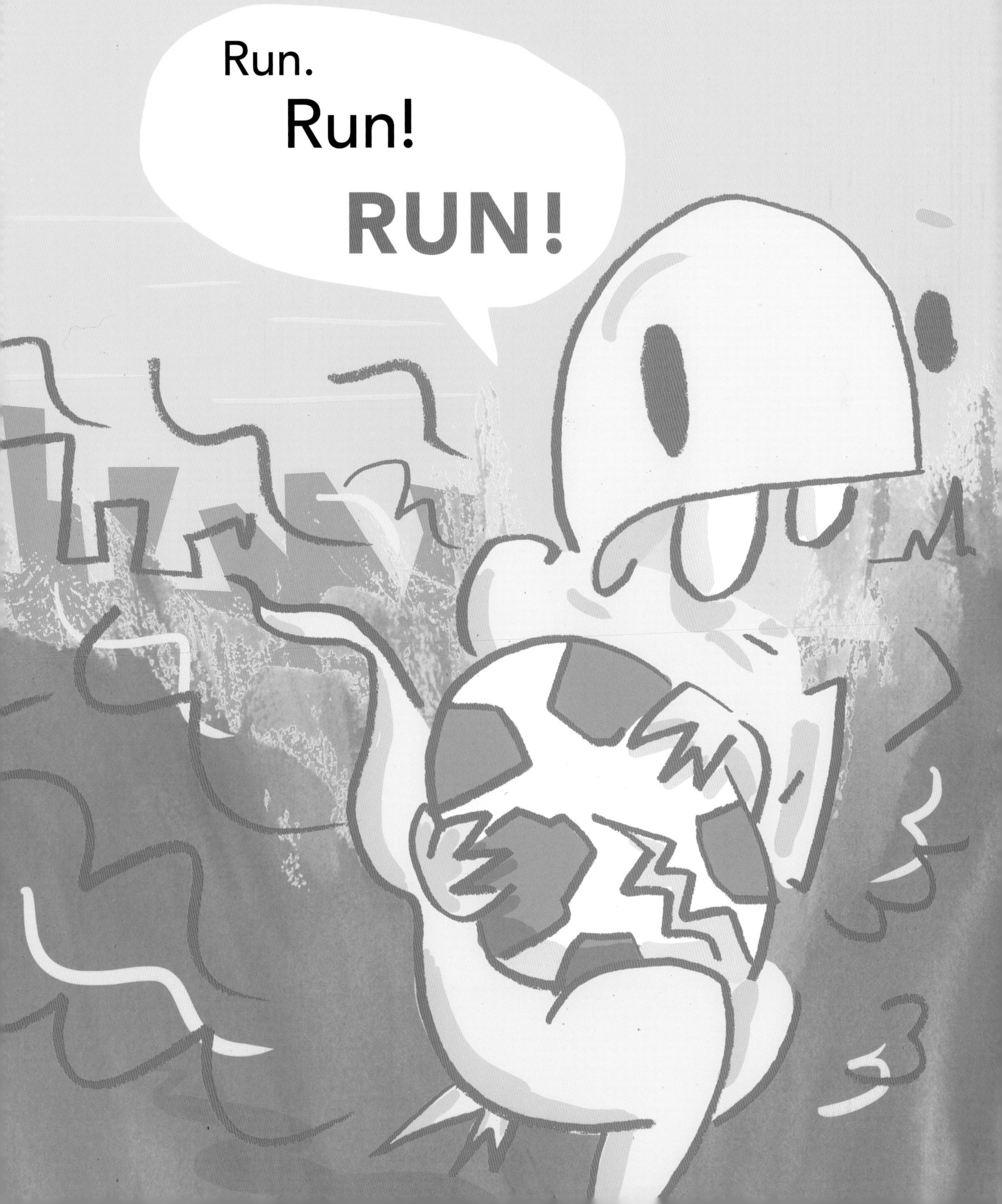

Rex floats.

Rex swoops.

Rex tumbles.

Rex bounces.

And Rex rolls.

And maybe a new . . .

Archelon!

Jaekelopterus!

Askeptosaurus!

Dunkleosteus!